DOUGLAS FORD

The Last Slaughter

This one is dedicated to Jerlin

Acknowledgement

A slightly different version of this novella appeared in TABLE FOR 3, a 2023 publication containing three novellas assembled together by Holly Rae Garcia in response to the growing crisis of food insecurity. Holly put a great deal of love and care into that volume, and its proceeds benefited a Texas food bank, proving once again that the horror often serves a higher purpose—in this case, helping to feed families. CAT FOOD, Holly's own contribution to TABLE FOR 3, can now be read in her collection of fiction, FLESH COMMUNION AND OTHER STORIES. Be sure to check out that book, along with Holly's other excellent work.

One

J ohn Teecar knew the truth, even if no one besides his mother, Laura, ever said it out loud: Pinky Randall was his father.

That Pinky Randall, the richest man in town. So rich that Laura Teecar's parents didn't require a chaperone when he came calling upon their daughter soon after she turned sixteen. Her birthday came in August, and the Swine Awards took place every Autumn. At least until food became scarce and the land went dry.

But in those days, before so many of them started going hungry, people owed their livelihoods to land-owners like the Randalls. Good stock came from that family, just like the beef they harvested in their slaughterhouses and the bacon cut from their fattened hogs. Who could blame Mr. and Mrs. Teecar if they thought that Pinky Randall had only the most honorable intentions with Laura?

John knew the story by heart—how Pinky Randall showed up in a shiny pink convertible and wearing polished wing-tip shoes, all untarnished by the blood floors of his family's killing rooms. He beamed at Mr. and Mrs. Teecar from where he sat on their living room sofa, his hands folded neatly in his lap. How they fussed over him, for having a member of the Randall family in one's living room practically amounted to playing host to royalty. John's grandmother, Mrs. Teecar, kept asking him over and over if he'd like a glass of sweet tea.

"No ma'am," Pinky Randall said each time, acting as if he'd heard the question for only the first time. "I'm saving room for the banquet. You do have such a nice home, Mr. Teecar."

John's grandfather smiled back from his usual place in his recliner. He sat on it every evening after coming home from a busy day of caring for livestock, often so tired that he fell asleep within moments of leaning back. He put in hard hours, but it kept food on the table in those days before everything went into decline. That didn't stop his expression from looking haunted at times. Understandable when you consider how his job involved spilling blood from living things, even calves newly separated from their mother for their fine meat. He would die just one year later, the result of a heart attack, but fortunately he lived long enough to see the birth of his bastard grandson. A good employee, he never breathed a word about what Pinky Randall did.

"I'm honored to hear those words," Mr. Teecar said. He didn't lean back in his recliner, not with such a refined visitor in his home. To do so would suggest disrespect, even if his age at 54 almost doubled that of his esteemed guest. A member of the Randall family might smile as if they did not perceive an insult, but rest assured they noticed every gesture and would find a way to redress any slight aimed in their direction. Mr. Teecar didn't want to find himself shoveling shit vacated from the bowels of dying animals. He knew that lowering the backrest of his chair and raising his feet could have that unintended consequence.

Smiling politely, Pinky Randall declined two more offers of a glass of sweet tea. Each new offer made by Mrs. Teecar made her husband flinch, for one could never reliably anticipate what might insult a member of the Randall dynasty, especially its heir.

In truth, Mr. and Mrs. Teecar could not wait for their daughter to emerge from her bedroom so that her date with this important man could finally commence and they could breathe easily again. When she eventually did appear, she stood before them wearing her pink communion dress, a choice made in honor of Pinky's name at the suggestion of her mother.

Evidently, that decision met his approval because Pinky smiled and licked his lips. "Why, you look fine, Laura. Almost as beautiful as your dear mother."

Mrs. Teecar blushed at this remark. Meanwhile, her husband broke out in sweat, his nervousness now painfully manifest.

"She's wearing that in honor of you," said Laura's mother. Then she repeated her statement as if no one heard her the first time, and the sweat on Mr. Teecar's forehead became all the more palpable.

"Well, now," said Pinky Randall, "I must make my own tribute in return. What shall that be?" He demonstrated his careful deliberation by wrinkling his brow and tapping his chin. Then he snapped his fingers. "I know! The hog I intend to enter into this year's swine competition. You know the animal I refer to, don't you, Ralph?"

Despite Mr. Teecar's seniority, Pinky Randall always referred to him by his first name. Ralph Teecar shifted in his seat, uncomfortable with the turn in direction just taken by the conversation. Of course he knew the hog, a prized specimen kept in a special pen. "I do," he finally said.

Pinky Randall's expression showed no evidence that he found

his host's hesitation too long or impolite. Still grinning, his eyes marched up and down Laura's fine form. He said, "I'll name that hog after your sweet daughter."

Quiet hung over the room. Perhaps no one knew what to say. Finally, Mrs. Teecar clapped her hands. "Well, isn't that an honor. It is, isn't it, Laura? You heard what Mr. Randall just said."

But Laura didn't speak. She regarded first her parents and then Pinky Randall with a blank expression. The sweat trickled down Mr. Teecar's forehead and burned his eyes. He fumbled in his pockets for a handkerchief, but he couldn't find one.

"What do you say to that, you fine thing?" asked Pinky Randall.

"What do you say to that, girl?" her father asked.

Though she mumbled, her words indistinct, no one missed the inflection at the end of her reply. But if that bothered Pinky Randall, he carried such good breeding that he didn't allow it to show. "Well now," he said, "we've got to be on our way." He offered his arm to Laura, and an awkward moment ensued when she hesitated, evidently not sure how to accept such a formal gesture, especially from a suitor with the grace and sophistication of Pinky Randall.

Laura's mother saw them to the door, and even Ralph Teecar rose from his recliner to shake the younger man's hand one last time. His palms felt moist, an obvious fact to everyone when Pinky Randall wiped his hand on his pants leg.

"Rest assured, I'll have her home at a respectable hour," said Pinky Randall just before opening the passenger door of his convertible and assisting Laura inside. Mr. and Mrs. Teecar waved as the car departed in a cloud of dust. Only then did they look at one another. Ralph Teecar saw the tears in his wife's eyes.

"Stupid fucking woman," he said.

He spoke these words in a growl so low that Mrs. Teecar thought she misheard him.When she turned to him, she saw a look of pure loathing in his expression.

"You just babbled like an idiot," he said. "Did you not understand the first time that the man *did not want your goddamn tea?*"

She hardly knew what to say. "I only asked him once," she said finally, though she knew she asked him many times. "Did I offend him?"

"*Did I offend him?* You most certainly did offend him." Feeling a slight pang in his chest—the first sign of the blockage that would kill him in just over a year—Ralph Teecar returned to his living room and slumped into his recliner.

"You did nothing to help the situation," Mrs. Teecar said. "All you did was sit there." She bit her lip. "If we truly offended Mr. Randall—"

"You mean, if *you* offended him," her husband said.

"—then he'll still bring Laura home on time, won't he? He won't... I mean, he'll bring her home, won't he?" She couldn't identify the ominous fear that came over her. She silently reminded herself of the pedigree of the Randall family. Pinky Randall had money, and people with money never did dishonorable things. Having money meant a blessing from the Lord, and He didn't bestow fortune on the unworthy or profane.

"Damn stupid woman," said Ralph Teecar. Then he used the television remote to turn on that evening's game show. Then they watched a series of sitcoms that failed to make either of them laugh, and finally, the evening news came on. Before long, they struggled to remain awake while Johnny Carson made jokes at the expense of the president. Not one word between them the entire time, even well after the respectable hour came and went without Pinky Randall's convertible appearing in their driveway.

Nor did they speak right away when Laura herself stumbled through the door, her face wet with tears and sweat. The torn strap of her pink dress hung from her bare shoulder, and the light of the television revealed her bleeding lips and blackened left eye. Later, while helping Laura undress and step into the shower, Mrs. Teecar saw the teeth marks on her daughter's breasts and the torn flesh between her thighs.

As he waited in the hallway, the sweats hit Ralph Teecar something awful. That fluttering in his chest felt out of control, and he dreaded the next time he would see Pinky Randall at work. For all he knew, he would find himself unemployed in the morning. "Stupid woman," he said once more, even though his wife stood outside the range of hearing as she helped her daughter clean off the blood and the dirt. "Goddamn stupid."

Two

Before he reached full adulthood, John Teecar knew these details by heart, and though he never had the opportunity to know him personally, he felt as if he had developed an intimate knowledge of his grandfather's personality. He held his memory in high regard, considering him a saint amongst men and too good to live long in this world. His grandfather spent his short life earning an honest living at Randall Meats, but all he had to show for it was a crumbling gravestone with his last name incorrectly spelled with two *r*'s instead of one:

Rudolph C. Teecarr
Loving Father and Husband
Faithful Employee of Randall Meats

"See that?" his mother would say on the occasions when they drove together to the cemetery to lay flowers upon his grandfather's final resting place. "That's the only thing that ties your daddy's name to yours." She drew upon her cigarette and released a long plume of smoke, a habit she developed a month after she gave birth to John Teecar, once she knew that the world would never show her any kindness. "Never doubt the truth, no matter how much they try to deny it. You are a Randall."

John picked up a sizeable chunk of gravestone that had broken away. Cheap granite, apparently, not even marble. Other fragments lay strewn on the grass, broken off as a result of some truancy, maybe a Halloween prank. He gripped the broken piece as he listened to his mother's pronouncement, one she repeated for as long as he could remember. Perhaps as early as a toddler, stumbling his way through the gravestones. As a gangly teenager, he began to grasp the significance of what his mother told him regarding his true parentage, especially as he bore witness to how the rest of the town bowed down before the privileged feet of the Randall legacy. That awareness evolved into resentment as he closed in on his twenties. Though only sixteen years his senior, his mother looked much older, thanks to the effects of poverty and the Pall Malls.

"I used to be pretty," she liked to tell him as he grew older. "You know that, right?"

"You're still pretty," he always said in reply.

"Bullshit," she'd say, but she would reach over and squeeze his shoulder.

After visiting the cemetery, they'd drive past the main processing building for Randall Meats. In recent years, it had grown quiet as the effects of a long drought persisted, the worst in several generations. For miles in every direction, one saw fields covered in dead grass and dried waterbeds.

Dust coated the air, which they now attributed to Laura's worsening cough. They rolled up the windows and suffered through the inside heat of the vehicle. Because of the coughing, John did most of the driving. "Go ahead and roll down your window," she said. "I'm going to cough either way. Damn allergies."

Both of them knew the coughing had nothing to do with

allergies.

"Let's go up a ways further. I want to see if anyone's tending your granddaddy's old post." Laura pointed toward an old service road, and John complied, though he thought he ought to get them home so she could rest. The longer they stayed out, the worse the coughing became.

The road took them to what looked like a series of out-buildings, where Ralph Teecar once oversaw the more prized livestock, including more than one winner of the Swine Awards. "There," Laura said once it came into view. "That's where it happened. Where you were conceived. Where Pinky Randall kept his prized pigs." She tried laughing, but that only resulted in more coughing. When it subsided, she said in a croaking voice, "Laura. He still named it after me, you know. The swine."

John nodded, though he didn't know if she referred to the animal or to Pinky Randall. He stared at the building, willing himself not to cry. He wanted to use his mother's lighter to set that building aflame, perform a mad dance as he watched it burn. His hands gripped the wheel, wondering if he could ever summon the courage to perform this act.

"Alright." Once more his mother squeezed his shoulder. "Time to go. Remember to keep the windows down." She lit another Pall Mall, and the car filled with smoke as they lumbered back up the service road. No air moved through the open windows. When they reached the intersection, John pressed the brake and let the car idle. Then he faced his mother.

"One more stop," he said.

She raised an eyebrow in reply, but she sensed what he had in mind. John turned right instead of left. He followed the curve of the county road until it brought them to a wooden fence. Beyond that, a line of oaks. On the former site of an antebellum plantation now sat a garish, three-story mansion. The gate that guarded his driveway hung open. John drove slowly so as not to arouse suspicion, aware that the old compact car made labored noises, its pistons and gears doomed to fail at any moment. *Just a little further. Don't die here*, he thought. His mother smoked as the Randall manor home came into view.

"Do what you're going to do fast," she said. "I don't want to be caught dead here." She flicked her cigarette out the window as John stopped the car. She watched him as he gripped the piece of broken granite from his grandfather's gravestone and exited the vehicle. She looked for cameras as John walked to within minimum distance of a plate glass window overlooking the driveway, where he reared back and threw the granite with all his might. Then came the sound of shattered glass and from somewhere distant, an alarm.

As John walked briskly back to the car, she lit another cigarette. They watched the dashboard with anticipation, wondering if the car would even start again. Laura exhaled smoke through her nostrils. "Next time, keep it running." John ignored the remark, trying a second time and then a third time. On the fourth try, the engine finally started, and they peeled away with a screech of the tires, the alarm still ringing behind them.

Three

Surprisingly, committing this lawless act did nothing to change how John felt about his circumstances. When they returned home, he saw the same squalor waiting them, a decades-old house fallen into disrepair due to lack of money and resources, as well as the same lifeless pasture and the same empty pantry, save what they could cobble together from food stamps and hand-outs at the local food bank. Even worse, they returned to the same mute occupant who shared the house with them: John's grandmother, limited to a sad existence in bed after the stroke she suffered on John's sixteenth birthday.

Though the stroke robbed her of speech and mobility, her heart continued to beat soundly and reliably, steadfast in its refusal to give up. John visited her daily, assisting her with her bodily needs and talking to her, sometimes answering for her when he asked her questions.

He sat near now while outside the window, his mother spoke to the deputy who showed up to inquire about the broken window at the Randall residence. Silently, he held his grandmother's hand in his lap, wondering if the deputy would take him to jail. His grandmother's hand squeezed his, though whether from reflex or sympathy, John couldn't tell.

Eventually, the deputy drove away, and his mother joined

him in the bedroom.

"We need to move her before she gets a new bedsore," Laura said. "Help me out."

John complied. As usual, he observed how his mother treated his grandmother with rough hands, grabbing and pinching without regard for the woman's comfort. He tried to balance that with extra gentleness. Without conversation, they adjusted the old woman's position, John waiting for her to report on what the deputy said. The possibility of jail made him anxious. Finally, her silence forced him to ask.

She snapped her reply at him. "No. You're not going to jail. Just get over yourself."

Though not a stranger to unexpected spikes in his mother's temper, they still hurt nonetheless, even when she softened quickly, as she did now.

"He wouldn't take you to prison," she said. "He's sweet on me. He just wanted to know if I wanted to go out to dinner with him this Saturday. I told him I had other gentleman callers." She smiled. "Don't you see them lining up outside?"

John forced himself to smile. "What did you really say?"

"He asked me if I was Laura Teecar. I said, 'Yeah, that's me. Pinky Randall's prized pig.' He said he was here to investigate an act of vandalism, and I said I didn't know anything about it. I told him to tell Pinky Randall to come face us like a man. I said that if he weren't a no-good coward that he could finally meet his son in person. Remind him, I said, that we live down the road and that he can come say hello himself rather than send some limp-dick deputy instead."

"Am I or am I not going to jail?"

"No, you're not going to jail. Pinky Randall doesn't have the balls to press charges. He'd have to face us. Face you."

Later, John found himself dozing on the recliner in front of the television. Each night he slept on the recliner that once belonged to Ralph Teecar, his usual spot since his grandmother had one room while his mother had the other. When it chose to work, the television provided him with a kind of lullaby every night, helping him shut out the rest of the world. Just before he could slip away into sleep, he heard a knock at the door.

Dressed only in his underwear, he answered and found the deputy on the other side of the door.

"You dress that way around your mother?" the deputy asked.

John pinched the fly of his boxers to keep them closed. "Hold on, I'll get my pants." He assumed the deputy came to take him to jail, but before he could get one leg into his trousers, his mother came into the room wearing a negligee he'd never in his life seen.

"You're late," she said to the deputy, who now stood inside the doorway, even though John sure as shit didn't invite him.

"Rufus Birdwell fell into his septic tank," said the deputy.

Laura looked at the deputy, and John looked at how much thigh her negligee revealed. "Do I know Rufus Birdwell?"

"Doesn't matter," the deputy said. "He's dead now. Methane killed him." The deputy looked at John. "Only takes three or four minutes of breathing it before it kills your brain. We had to fish him out. I needed a shower."

"Very considerate of you." Laura motioned to her son. "Turn up that TV." Then she led the way to her room, the deputy glancing back at John with a shit-eating grin.

John didn't turn up the volume of the television. Instead, he endured every gasp, every moan, every sigh that came from his mother's room, and he didn't sleep a wink all night. A just punishment, he decided, considering that he could only blame himself for throwing that cheap piece of granite.

He just wished it hit someone when he threw it and split their skull open.

Four

After some time, he decided he couldn't take any more and that he needed to leave. He had a destination in mind, too. If he had to serve some form of penance, he would do something that truly warranted it. Upon getting dressed, he took the car keys, and after considering it for a few moments, he also took his mother's cigarette lighter. Before driving off, he went into their run-down shed and found some cloth rags, along an old metal gas container he used to fill the lawn mower on the occasions that it worked.

Then he left quickly just to make sure he wouldn't have to see the deputy's shit-eating grin again. If he saw the man's face again, he might pound it into a pulpy mess. Then it wouldn't matter who his mother decided to fuck. Nothing he could do about it from a jail cell.

Or Death Row. Jail scared him, but nothing froze his blood like the thought of Death Row.

As he drove toward his destination, he thought of what his mother said to him once. *We do for family what we sometimes wouldn't do for just ourselves.* Maybe that explained the disgusting act she decided to perform with the deputy. Not for herself—how could she possibly desire the deputy of all people?—but for him.

Somehow that only seemed to enrage him more. It made him feel guilty. And dirty.

To get rid of those feelings, he needed to do something for her.

As he used his last ten dollars to fill the gas can, he watched the moon climb up over the horizon and into a cloudless sky. Then he drove toward Randall Meats, his father's empire as well as his birthright, though he would never inherit it. His route took him once more past his grandfather's final resting place.

Along the way, he considered burning down Pinky Randall's house, but he decided against it, balking at the idea of killing the people inside it. He didn't know for certain, but he suspected that Pinky kept a staff, probably a butler and gaggle of maids that answered to his every whim and need. Killing them would surely hand him on Death Row, and he wouldn't have a single argument to make in his own defense. *Yeah, I did it,* he'd say to the judge before the gavel fell. And they'd catch him for sure. After the window incident, Pinky probably installed cameras everywhere.

Instead, he considered burning down Randall Meats itself, that concrete monstrosity overlooking a dead land. He suspected that it stood empty now, many of its employees let go in the name of downsizing. With feed becoming scarcer and more expensive, so did meat products, and everyone except the very wealthy slowly starved in a dwindling environment. The apocalypse could not happen fast enough for John. If the planet was burning like they said (and John had no reason to doubt it), then it sure was taking its damn time. Better to just have a rock fall from space and kill everyone all at once.

In the end, he decided to leave Randall Meats standing. He

suspected his ten dollars couldn't buy enough gasoline to bring down the whole thing, and he truly did want a fiery spectacle and as much devastation as he could buy with American money.

Then he got a better idea: that outbuilding where his grandfather once worked. Where *it* happened. Where Pinky Randall violated his mother and planted the seed that would one day become John.

He made the turn and soon enough came in sight of his target. It sat dark and quiet, probably like the day Pinky took his mother to see his prized pig, the one he named in her "honor."

John heard the story enough times that he knew it by heart— how Pinky talked on and on about that pig as he drove his mother to the banquet dinner, where all the other big-wigs in the food industry gathered for a giant feast so they could compare their respective bank accounts. Laura still found herself disbelieving that Pinky would choose her as his date, and she could barely contain herself as she thought about the smorgasbord awaiting her. At the time, Laura loved food, but hated enduring her mother's criticisms of her appetites. *Don't eat so much or you'll get fat. Then no man will marry you,* Laura's mother used to say. And Laura believed it, just as she once believed she would one day find happiness through marriage. Maybe she allowed herself to imagine nuptials with Pinky Randall himself.

Pinky promised Laura they would make it a short stop. She had no interest in meeting a pig, especially one not already prepared for feasting. Having one named after her certainly didn't make it special. No way did it make *her* feel special. If anything, she ought to feel insulted, but this date and what it symbolized meant so much to her parents, and she didn't want to disappoint them. She especially wanted to avoid her father's disappointment, though she never specified the reason for that.

In those days, Laura struggled to express herself, a problem she no longer experienced. John could count as truth whatever words passed through her lips, or so he reflected as he stopped the car a safe distance away and began gathering the rags along with the gas can. He imagined how the scene would have looked all those years ago, Pinky stopping his convertible on this very spot and taking Laura by the hand. *Only a few minutes, you'll see,* he likely promised as he led her to the entrance of the outbuilding. According to Laura, she'd come to this building before a few times prior to this occasion, always in the company of her mother to bring her father something he'd forgotten, often his lunch, but he never allowed her to see what they kept on the inside. Her father always met them at the car, and if Laura expressed any desire to see the interior of the building, he would shake his head impatiently. *You can't,* he'd say, *Mr. Randall won't allow it. You can't even tell anyone you've been here.* Then he'd look at his wife meaningfully. *I might get fired.*

John imagined how these words would have wounded Laura's daughterly devotion. She craved her father's attention. When she found him fast asleep on his recliner, she would sometimes crawl in next to him, snuggling close to him all the way until the morning sun rose. How it must have offended her to see her father keep something so private, not even opening the door for her to take even a peek, but standing there waving at them until they finally drove away.

Undoubtedly, Laura kept these occasions to herself as Pinky Randall unlocked this very door so that she could gaze upon his special pig. How special? Pinky couldn't wait for her to see. He winked at her as he invited her to step inside.

Was there even a pig? John pondered this question as

he trudged up a short incline, arms weighed down by his supplies. His mother's answer to this question always involved inconsistencies. Sometimes she claimed to have seen the swine just before Pinky wrestled her to the ground, and she found the animal unimpressive. Other times she confessed that she could see very little, though she sensed other eyes watching as she finally managed to fight her way out from underneath Pinky's weight, eventually stumbling outside with him calling after her. She stayed away from the road as she made the perilous trek home, avoiding headlights and the sound of tires, believing that Pinky would come after her with the intention of doing her serious harm.

Recollecting this story, John determined that he'd chosen his target correctly. A quiet stillness hung over the scene and burning down this horrid place would bring a certain symbolic satisfaction both to him and to his mother. He would also avoid, he believed, serious legal jeopardy. If the deputy came to arrest him, John would pose a simple question: why on earth would he burn down such a useless building? Of course, his mother had her own way of handling the deputy, but he wanted to avoid that. He hated thinking of his hands all over her.

Wooden boards covered the few windows on the main side of the building. Each piece of plywood bore strange markings, a strange sort of graffiti by the look of it, certainly not in a language he recognized—just loops, lines, and dots, denoting a symbolism foreign to his intelligence. Perhaps gang markings, though he knew of no gangs in their community. When he stepped closer to examine it more closely, the sound of crunching came from beneath his feet. He stepped back, thinking he'd stepped in glass, but it looked like something else. Sand perhaps, or more likely rock salt. Someone tossed heaps of salt along the outside the building, even in front of the door. That door, he assumed, would be locked, but he had no interest in testing that assumption.

Instead, he began soaking the rags in gasoline. Then he stuffed them between the boards and the cheap siding of the building. He'd never burned down a building, so he acted on instinct rather than knowledge or experience. The rags, he figured, would act as wicks, and once he had them spaced well enough, he would light them while giving his legs enough time to carry him far enough away to avoid any potential injury—but not too far that he couldn't enjoy the spectacle.

As he finished soaking the last rag, he thought he heard a voice calling out from the distance. Impulsively, he ducked. Crouching, he waited in anticipation, hopeful that it was just his nerves playing tricks on his senses.

When he heard nothing more, he quickly emptied the rest of the gasoline onto the salt heaped around the doorway, no longer putting any thought or deliberation into his actions. He needn't have bothered with the rags, he decided. He spent so much time wedging them in place. On the other hand, he needed something to ignite with the lighter, so they served their purpose. He took out his mother's lighter and started to flick its wheel.

But he heard the voice again. No more doubting the accuracy of his senses.

A woman's voice, calling for help.

He stood frozen, the lighter gripped in his right hand, trying to determine its source. He waited as the seconds ticked by, knowing somehow that he would hear it again. And he did.

"Help me."

Now he knew its point of origin—from behind one of the

boarded windows, someone pleading for help.

No telling what Pinky Randall used the building for nowadays. As far as John could tell, it stood in disrepair, dilapidated, even if it once housed the pigs Pinky used to win his collection of Swine Awards, including one such animal named Laura. He had no reason to believe that the owner of that voice posed a threat to him. On the contrary, they needed his help.

"Where are you?" he called out. "Keep talking." He moved past the stinking rags, waiting for a reply.

"Trapped in here," said the voice. "Let me out."

Now John could tell—it came from the plywood covering the last window. Once more, something crunched under his feet as he pressed his ear against the barrier. From the other side, he imagined he could hear sounds of desperate breathing.

"I'm going to get you out," he said, and he began pacing back and forth, not at all sure how he would manage that feat. Then he remembered—the car, parked a short distance away, contained what he needed: a spare tire accompanied by a heavy bar of iron. "Wait here," he said to whoever called out to him from inside the building.

Not that the person could go *anywhere* without his help. Probably someone kept prisoner by Pinky Randall, he reckoned. Maybe someone he kept chained to the wall, forced to endure perverted acts.

As he stumbled toward the car, he forgot all about the lighter and the gasoline. At least until lightning filled the sky. He reminded himself that it almost never rained anymore, the land around them so dry and brittle that hardly anything grew there, hastening the decline of Randall Meats.

Which would be just fine with him, if not for the fact that it meant everyone else in the community would slide deeper into poverty. That never seemed to change Pinky's circumstances though, living in that fine house up the street.

Once more lightning filled the sky, and John felt a twinge of fear as he reached the car. What if a bolt of lightning struck the building, igniting the gasoline and causing it to go up in flames with the woman stuck inside it? He found the tire iron and hastened his return, flinching with each lightning flash.

"I'm back!" he called out as he began working to pry loose the board, the sand or the salt or whatever grating beneath his shoes. As he labored, he noticed something else about the strange designs scrawled on the wood. Whoever put them there used, not paint but charcoal. He never heard of a gang that used such material. One good rainstorm and it would all come off.

Then again, what rain? he thought.

At first, he didn't think he'd ever pry the board loose. Someone used bolts rather than simple nails.

"Get me out of here," he heard the voice say.

It sounded more like a girl than a woman. He renewed his efforts with greater determination. Why didn't someone like him come to his mother's rescue all those years ago when Pinky defiled her? Where were the good people when you needed them?

Right here, he said to himself. *You're one of the good people.* Then he made one more pull, and finally, the board came free with a groan.

He pushed it aside so he could assess the next obstacle.

And he saw none. Just an opening that might have once held a stall door of some sort.

Darkness spilled from the opening. Even a flash of heat lightning did nothing to dispel it.

All thoughts of leaping in heroically fell to the wayside.

Instead, he hesitated.

He spoke to the darkness. "You in there?"

"Yes," came the response. A quiet voice, almost as if she now feared him. And maybe she had good reason for mistrusting a stranger. He shuddered to imagine what she experienced in there.

"I'm going to save you," he said.

But the darkness coiled around him, and he failed to move.

"Okay," said the voice.

That spurred him into motion. He stepped over the line of salt and into the building.

Under his feet, the floor felt pliant. Hay, he surmised. Unable to see, he fumbled again for the lighter, but the flame did little to dispel the darkness.

What he could see looked unkept and in disrepair, the hay filthy. The noxious odor of human waste rose around him, and he unsuccessfully tried to stifle it by covering his nose.

The buzzing of flies led him to a corner where he found the girl.

Her appearance in the lighter's flame startled him. Not simply because of her nakedness, but also the insects that hovered about her, attracted by her filth, as well as the odor that he now knew originated with her. She huddled there with her knees drawn up to her chest, and her huge black eyes glittered in the light cast by his flame. Tangled hair lay matted against her skull, but he still felt his loins stirring in her presence. He wondered what sort of monster could keep a human being imprisoned in such squalor. Of course, he knew the answer: a monster like Pinky Randall. He thanked his mother's lucky stars that at least she'd escaped.

"Hungry," the girl said, extending her hand. "So hungry."

"Can you walk?"

She shook her head.

Fortunately, John inherited the strength and hardiness of his mother's side of the family. He managed to lift the girl into his arms, averting his eyes to avoid any unbecoming gaze upon her naked form, but also because of the rankness of her odor.

With his mother's lighter stowed away again, the darkness gathered unabated, and he found himself stumbling blindly, trying to locate the exit.

He felt her hot breath on his neck as he meandered through the hay.

"I know you," she said.

How could she possibly know him? How could she even see him? Maybe she'd developed exceptional night vision thanks to her imprisonment.

When he didn't answer, she said, "You'll feed me. No one's fed me in a long time, and I'm so, so hungry."

"I'll feed you," he said. "And we'll get you cleaned up."

Despite her unhygienic state, John's arousal only increased due to the oily warmth of her skin. His arms began to ache, and his knees started to wobble, despite how light she was. Clearly, Pinky Randall intended her to starve to death in that building.

Before his legs could surrender, he found the way out. More lightning illuminated the sky as they met the night air. John could breathe deeply again, his lungs filling with fresh air. Still carrying the girl, he hobbled toward the car, where he set her gently in the passenger seat. Though the car's interior light made her naked form starkly visible, he still buckled the seat belt for her and did his best not to touch her in a compromising way. "I'm sorry that I don't have a blanket or anything," he said.

She simply watched him with those big eyes of hers as he

pressed buckle into place. He avoided returning her gaze, though he felt her continuing to watch him as he walked around the car to get behind the wheel.

He paused with the door open, looking back toward the building. More lightning flashes, but still no rain. Nor, he well knew, would they see any.

"Wait here. Just a minute," he said to the girl sitting in the passenger seat.

As he walked back toward the building, he removed the lighter from his pocket. He kept looking back toward the car, making sure that the girl listened to what he said and didn't try to follow him or run away. He could see her still sitting there, her position unchanged. He continued to monitor her as he stepped up to one of the gasoline-soaked rags.

One more glance back to see her not only sitting there, but her head turned, watching him. He liked that. He wanted someone to see what he intended to do.

Then he lit the rag.

Five

They spoke little as he drove, the long silences broken only when he tried to find out her name. She didn't seem to have one. Or she had many. The first time he asked, she muttered something he struggled to pronounce back to her. *Tonacacihautl,* she said, but his tongue tripped over the syllables. Then she said *Erecura,* a name that sounded a little less foreign to his ears, but before he could repeat it, she added others. *Tari Pennu. Demeter.* He finally concluded that she suffered from some sort of delirium, or maybe she just wanted to fuck with him.

Behind them, the night lit up with an orange glow, the flames he set into motion now fully engulfing the building.

Trying to keep his eyes averted from her nudity, he considered her features, wondering if she crossed the border as a migrant worker. Maybe she feared he would turn her over to federal agents for deportation.

"I wouldn't do that," he said out loud without specifying what he meant.

Her eyes met his. Embarrassed, he returned his gaze to the road.

"I mean I wouldn't hand you over to the authorities, if that's what you're worried about. Me and them don't get along too well. There's a certain deputy I hate, for one thing. I won't turn you over to Pinky Randall, either. We don't have an official sheriff, so he just acts like one, bossing everyone around. You can tell me your real name, if you want."

She reached over and touched his knee, causing him to flinch. He tried to concentrate on the driving. Something nagged at him. Did he forget something?

"Hungry," she said, but she didn't try to touch his knee again. She spoke softly, as if a prolonged period of silence made her vocal cords ache. "Starving."

"I know. I just need to get you someplace safe."

He counted on finding the deputy's car gone by the time he made it home, and he breathed a sigh of relief when he saw no sign of that mother-defiling idiot. Dawn began to break. Faintly, he smelled smoke, and that made him feel good. From somewhere far off he heard a siren. Maybe the deputy got called in to investigate the fire he set. He felt relieved that he had not set the building aflame with the girl inside it. That would have made him guilty of murder, a crime almost equal in weight to all the terrible things Pinky Randall had done, especially when you added human trafficking.

Still not knowing what to call her (*Tari? Demeter?*), he helped the girl out the car, wondering if she would ever come clean with him regarding her circumstances. Or if she would simply die. Severe hunger made her profoundly weak, but she seemed to have recovered the ability to walk at least, though he still had to assist her up the front steps and into the house. She paused at the threshold to look behind them at the dead pasture overlooking the home, visible now in the gloom of dawn. "My family used to farm here," he said. "A long time ago. Can't grow nothing here now. Not anymore. Everything's dried up and dead."

Whether or not that information made an impression, he couldn't tell. He wondered if he ought to clean her up before he tried to feed her, but once inside, she made the decision for him, hobbling to the kitchen table, bare-assed and filthy. What his mother would say if she found them like that, he could only imagine. He decided it didn't matter, so he began opening and closing cupboards, not surprised at all when he found little more than a bowl of sugar and a stale bread loaf. Even from a distance, the girl's odor proved strong, earthy and faintly metallic, like blood, but it no longer offended him. So he placed the bread and sugar in front of her and sat down in the adjacent chair.

At that moment, it hit him. What nagged him. What he'd forgotten.

"Goddammit," he said, and he struck the table with his fist.

The girl didn't react, though she watched him as he pressed his face into his hands. The bread and sugar sat untouched before her.

"I left the fucking tire iron," he said, finally. "I left it sitting there for them to find."

Rendered immobile by his own ineptness, he wondered if the flames would reach a temperature hot enough to melt iron. He doubted it.

Then he saw the way his table companion watched him, and the blankness of her expression infuriated him. Did she feel pity for him, or maybe he detected something mocking in those large eyes, almost too big for her face. Then he saw the food that sat ignored before her.

"I thought you were so goddamn hungry," he said. "Why the fuck don't you eat?" His voice sounded harsher than he intended, but she didn't so much as flinch, and somehow that made him angrier. He swept everything on the table to the floor, the bowl of sugar shattering to bits on the cheap linoleum. She regarded the mess on the floor with a neutral expression, as if observing a curious though unremarkable phenomenon.

Then she stood and walked out of the house.

For a moment, John just sat there, his fists clenched. How hot would it have to get for iron to melt? Still no clue. And what about the tires of the car? They left tracks, and he knew from the television that no longer worked how the authorities could match those to the car that made them.

Thoughts swirled in his head, and he almost didn't care where the girl had gone.

Then it mattered. He'd saved her, after all. At the very least, she owed him her silence.

He rushed out the door and saw her standing in the pasture. After making him carry her earlier, it turned out that she could move quite well. All an act, apparently.

He called out to her. "Hey!" But she didn't turn. Nor did she make an effort to run. She just stood there like a statue, a forgotten idol in a barren landscape, her form silhouetted in the growing light of morning.

As he made his way toward her, a peculiar feeling came over him, as if he'd stepped into the presence of something ethereal, eternal, transcendent. Maybe not those words exactly, but their ineluctable effects. His steps slowed as he came closer, the naked skin of her back glistening with perspiration.

Sensing his approach, she turned, and he saw that she held a shard taken from the broken sugar bowl. He reached for her, but she acted faster, taking his wrist and using the shard to slice into the palm of his hand.

He tried to wrench his hand away, but she held him firmly. She twisted his wrist so that the blood dripped into the dust near their feet.

He stared at her in horror as her chapped lips formed a smile. "This is what I'm hungry for." Then she pressed his hand to her face, and he felt her tongue probing the wound, licking it. When she let his arm fall away, he saw his blood smearing her face. She smiled wickedly now, her teeth so white they looked predatory. "I know you," she said, repeating the words she muttered when he carried her to the car.

As they stood there in the desolation of the pasture, Laura stepped forth from the house. From a distance, she watched the two of them in silence.

Six

Years ago, after her date with Pinky Randall changed her life forever, Laura struggled to care about anything. She barely finished school, ignoring assignments and homework, with one notable exception.

Hoping to instill an appreciation for how their community depended upon the food industry and the benevolence of Randall Meats, a teacher assigned Laura's class with a project to learn about traditions involving food. After all, Thanksgiving loomed on the horizon, and the teacher assumed that the students would write something nice about Pilgrims or Indians. But Laura surprised everyone by looking into something much more remote, unusual, and disturbing.

But Laura wrote her report on the *troksoi* system, a practice that affected people in faraway African nations like Togo and Ghana. Laura would never have learned about this system if not for a lonely girl who appeared at their school one morning, only to find herself instantly shunned by nearly everyone—except Laura, who felt like a pariah herself, if for different reasons. Besides, Laura thought it was stupid to dislike a person because of a dark complexion. Apparently in need of asylum, the new girl somehow found her way to their rural community, whether through clerical mistake or some act of official cruelty, no one knew. Either way, she faced endless bigotry and harassment, but that only made Laura more sympathetic.

From her new friend, Laura, learned about how under the *troksoi* system, female children as young as seven years old would be taken away from their families, usually to punish their parents for a crime like adultery. These children would lose their clothes, their selfhood, and even their name to become the wife of the gods. Forced to live inside a shrine, they would serve the priests of a deity such as *Nyigbla*. Such a deity would bless the community with bountiful food, but only after the sacrifice of the *troksoi*.

In her report, Laura wrote, "Offending these gods brings misfortune. If you expect them to give you food and wine, you need to offer them sacrifices, if not in blood then in isolation."

For her report, Laura received a D, her teacher noting that such things only happened in uncivilized places, and ought not Laura count her blessings that she lived in a place where people enjoyed the freedom to work for their own prosperity?

Now, as she sat in her own kitchen, Laura studied this girl found by John, this girl who seemed to have no proper name, and she recalled how she crumpled up that report and threw it in the trash. She wondered what became of that teacher in subsequent years. If she suffered some malady and became a human vegetable like her mother, Laura would not waste a single tear on her. If this was prosperity, Laura didn't want any more of it. And as for the classmate who told her about the *troksoi* system? She disappeared, simply failing to show up for school one day. Laura never learned if she was relocated or decided to run away on her own.

And she hadn't thought about her in years, but now she wondered if John unwittingly rescued the victim of something similar—not in far off Ghana, but right here in their backyard.

But so far, the girl avoided answering their questions. She gazed back at John and Laura, her face indecipherable. Laura managed to get her covered with one of her mother's old bathrobes. Not that her nudity seemed to overly distract John, especially after that cutting episode. They managed to stop the bleeding, but Laura had to keep reminding him to keep his hand raised.

"Why exactly did you go into that godforsaken building?" she asked.

She listened as John told her again about how he just wanted another look at it. She still didn't understand why he went there without her. Then he added something he hadn't told her yet. "I heard her calling for help from inside."

"Calling for help, you say."

John didn't reply.

"So you can talk," said Laura to the mute girl. "If you can call out for help, you can say something to me."

A half-smile formed on the girl's lips. "I know you."

"That's what she said to me," said John.

"You know *me*? Or just him?" asked Laura. Distracted, John lowered his bleeding hand, and Laura brusquely raised it for him.

"I know you both," the girl said, still with that half-smile.

"You know us both *from where*? We don't know you at all."

No response, though the half-smile persisted. Laura sensed something uncanny in it, as if the girl really did know them, though from where, Laura had no idea. The fact that she came from that out-building that symbolized everything that had gone wrong with her life made Laura wary.

"Why were you there?" John started to answer, but Laura

shushed him. "From your lips," she said to the girl.

But before she could answer, someone knocked on the door with enough force that it shook in its frame.

"John Teecar," said the deputy from other side. "I'm here for you. And your mama ain't going to protect you this time."

John's hand fell again, but Laura didn't bother with lifting it this time. "What did you do?"

She stood before John could answer and headed for the door, not sure if she should open it or try to bar the deputy's way. The girl remained seated, her half-smile fixed and mocking.

Hesitating briefly, John removed his mother's lighter from his pocket and showed her, his face gone white.

"Oh, Jesus," she said. "Lock the door behind me." She opened the door, and before the deputy could react, she stepped through and shut it behind her. She prepared herself to feel the deputy's hands on her. She knew from the night before that he'd never heard of tenderness.

Instead, he rocked back on his heels, a hitch in his stance, like a regular Clint Eastwood. In one hand, he held a tire iron, and she wondered if he intended to use it to hammer down the door.

"Looks like you lost something," he said, gesturing with the crowbar.

Laura tried not to let her uncertainty show. She did her best to glower.

"Don't know what you're talking about. We don't own a crowbar."

He used it to point toward her car, which John left parked at a funny angle. "Came from there, I'm willing to bet. Your son used it to vandalize private property. Then he burned it to the ground."

Laura almost stopped herself from groaning out loud. "Not John. He was here all night."

The deputy laughed and pretended to watch something in the distance. "Yeah, well, when I left, the car wasn't around. The call came in on the drive home, and my first thought was, 'Hmm, I wonder where that car went.' Left some clear tracks behind, too. Bet I could match them to those tires and not even worry about this." He lifted the crowbar and rested it on his shoulder, no longer Clint Eastwood and now Reggie Jackson.

Laura considered asking for it back if he didn't need it. She decided it best to wait out his silence with her own.

"The thing is," said the deputy, "Mr. Randall has a soft spot for you all. He's willing to overlook the destruction of his private property—on one condition." Once more, he gazed into the distance, and this time, he seemed to get lost in thought. Then his eyes lit up as if he noticed something for real this time. "You get yourself a hog?"

"What?" She truly had no idea what he meant, but she didn't want to step away from the door, suspecting a ruse to draw her away so that he could push his way inside. Their land had not supported any livestock in generations, and their finances had fallen so low that they couldn't afford the cost. If Walmart showed up to buy their property for a superstore, she wouldn't be able to sign the papers fast enough. But even they knew a dying community when they saw one.

The deputy shook his head. "Probably a wild boar. But I haven't seen one in years."

"Get on with what you were saying," said Laura.

Unaccustomed to commands from a woman, especially one who whored around, the deputy glowered. "Mr. Randall would like his property returned to him. John took something that belongs to him, and he wants it back. Return it, and he won't file charges. Pretty generous, if you ask me. Like I said, he has a soft spot for your family."

It took every ounce of control to keep herself rooted to her spot and not step away from the door to rip off the deputy's dick. She could not, however, stop what came out of her mouth. "Fuck you. Fuck him, too." Spittle flew from her mouth and clung to her chin. She did not wipe it away. If she did, the tears might follow, and she did not cry in front of anyone. Not anymore.

The deputy nodded. "Mr. Randall speculated you might say that. He might come out himself, and you'll hear all this straight from the horse's mouth."

After one more glance in the direction of the pasture, he got into his car and drove away.

Laura waited, making sure he left the driveway and made it to the main road. Then she stepped away from the door and looked toward what drew the deputy's attention.

She saw it—a pig, and a young one by the look of it, but still round in the belly. Well-fed and healthy, from what she could see. Its hide consisted of a pattern of brown and white fur. It hunkered over the spot where John and the girl stood not long before—by the looks of it, in the very place where the blood from John's hand fell. With its snout buried in the ground there, the pig fed heartily.

Seven

oments afterwards, she and John would circle the animal carefully, each with a lassoed rope in their respective hands, careful so as not to scare it away. Perhaps because of its youth, the pig showed no concern over their approach, nor did it wander off as she feared it would when they went looking for rope.

It had taken work to motivate John to come out of the house. Through the window, he observed the exchange between her and the deputy, and he met her with lamentations when she returned inside.

"Quit sniveling and come out here with me," she said.

He denied sniveling, but Laura wouldn't have it. She didn't know when she would find it in her to forgive him for setting the fire, but that discussion would have to wait until they did something about the pig that wandered onto their property. His reaction to seeing it mirrored her own.

He said, "Could be others nearby, including its parents. I don't care to feel the wrath of a wild boar."

"Just find us some rope," said Laura. "Ought to be some in the shed."

"What about her?" They'd left the girl sitting inside. After the deputy's visit, Laura only had more misgivings about what her son brought home, but she decided to keep them to herself for the time being. Something about the girl felt so wrong, and it gave her the heebie-jeebies when she said that she *knew* them.

"She's not going anywhere," Laura said, ignoring the premonition that came over her, the unsettling sense that they might eventually wish that she hadn't entered their lives in the first place.

John found the two coiled lengths of rope, barely eight feet long each, but they would have to do. Miraculously, the pig made no effort to evade them, remaining fixed to the spot of ground it had chosen to gorge upon. Apparently, something bloomed in the earth where John's blood spilled. The pig offered little objection when they led it away and tied it to an old fence post between the shed and the house. The whole thing struck them both as nothing short of miraculous.

Thinking of her conversation with the deputy, Laura said, "This animal follow you home from your little adventure?"

John shook his head, but his eyes looked faraway, lost in thought.

"Because," Laura said, "they think you stole something from your father."

"It's her," said John. "I rescued her. She was like you. A *prisoner.*"

That premonition again. "She's not like me. I wasn't a prisoner."

"We should name the pig," John said. "If we're going to keep it. I vote for Pinky."

She had to fight back the urge to slap him. She began to fret over how long they'd left the girl inside by herself. "Let's get back in," she said, and they left the pig alone and unnamed, but tethered at least, standing dumbly in the sun.

Inside, they found the girl's seat empty.

"Maybe she slipped out through a window," John said, and he marched toward the rear of the house, as if he planned to stop her from getting away. For a rare moment, Laura wondered if her son inherited some of his father's more unsavory characteristics. She shook it off, reminding herself that John mirrored her best self, that for all her limitations, she raised him correctly. Still, it made her uneasy to see him act so possessively of what did not belong to him. As he stood gazing out an open window, it dawned on Laura where the girl might have gone.

"Shut that window," she said. "She's in here."

They went to her mother's bedroom, where they found the girl sitting beside the catatonic woman.

Except that her mother now looked more awake and aware. Her eyes blinked around the room. They moved from the girl to Laura and then back to the girl. Her mouth twitched as if she intended to say something, but the muscles in her face would not obey her commands. The girl held the old woman's hand, which trembled as if it would reject the contact if it only had the strength.

The girl smiled at her and then at Laura.

"You like your gift?" the girl asked.

"Gift?" John's voice came from behind Laura. His eyes peered over her shoulder and into the room. She felt him wanting to get past her, but she remained in the doorway, barring his passage. He wanted the girl. Laura harbored no doubt about that.

"The animal," said the girl. "He's yours to have." Her big eyes sparkled. "I want the heart. You bring me the heart, and I'll bestow more."

"More what?" Laura asked.

Instead of answering, the girl said, "You don't remember me, but I remember you. I thought that he brought you for me, a ripe, fertile, unsullied body. Then I smelled what you had in you. So I stayed back and watched as he took you for himself, right there in the hay. Then you ran away. And he left me there to starve."

Laura didn't speak. She couldn't find the words. She watched the girl's attention move away from her and toward her mother. The old woman looked like she would recoil if her body would only allow it, her gaze fixed with an expression of both wonder and horror as the girl stroked her hand.

"She acts like she doesn't know," said the girl to the older, stricken woman, "but you and I both do, and we know who put it in her. She still smelled so pretty and fresh, but I knew she wouldn't taste right, so I let her run away. I left it growing inside her."

Laura realized what she meant by *it*. John. She meant John.

"You get away from her." The words left Laura's mouth without her volition, the manifestation of rage that precedes reason and deceit. "You get away from all of us."

"You're not the first to live on this land," the girl said, "and you won't be the last. I've been with the first people, and I'll still be here when the sun finally gets tired and burns out. In the meantime, do what I say. Save the animal's blood, and bring me an offering. Its heart."

With her free hand, she opened the dying woman's nightgown, and she used a fingernail to draw a circle over the gray, mottled skin stretched like parchment over her sternum. Laura watched her mother's chest rise and fall quickly as the fingernail left behind an angry red mark, along with a spot of blood.

Eight

I n defiance, they decided to let the pig escape. However, it demonstrated no inclination to run away. Even when they untied the rope from around its neck, it showed them no fear, merely sauntering back to the spot in the pasture where John's blood fell into the earth, once more burying its snout into the ground. Despite its feral appearance, it behaved like a contented, domesticated animal, a miracle if they ever saw one. They had no choice but to keep the animal, so once more they used the rope to tie it to the fence post. They watched it in silence as they pondered what they ought to do.

"What did she mean?" John finally asked.

Laura regarded him and pretended to not know what he meant.

"All that talk about smelling you. And someone putting something in you. I can barely say it." His mouth twisted as he spoke, his face like the one he made as a little boy when forced to drink cough syrup. Something inside her wanted to touch his face and wrap her arms around him, hugging him like a child she would never let go. "She's talking about Pinky Randall, right? She can't know about that."

"She's making things up," Laura said. "She doesn't know what she's talking about."

John gestured toward the animal tied before them. It regarded them back, their indecision about its fate nothing more than a minor indisposition. "It's a good animal," said John. "Healthy. Got meat on its bones. I can't see us just letting it go."

No reply from Laura. She watched the animal watching them.

John couldn't wait out her silence. "I say we let her have its heart. She's just crazy, so what hurt would it do? Is that what you think, too?"

Now she turned to him. "Do I think what?"

"That she's crazy." He tried smiling at her, but the effort only made him look like his father, and for the first time, Laura felt afraid of him. She studied his features, looking for signs of Pinky Randall in her son.

"She's something. Find a good metal bucket and take him to the shed. Do what she said. Make sure you catch all its blood."

"All of it?"

"Just do like she said. You know how to cut it."

"It's in my DNA," John said. Without another word, he took the animal's rope. "Come along, Pinky," he said as he led the pig away.

Laura watched them go, wincing at the name.

Nine

The animal remained pliant, giving John no trouble. Not only did it allow John to lead it to the shed, but it offered no resistance when he tied together its back feet. Soon, John had it suspended upside down. It hardly grunted, and when John used a knife to slice its thick neck, it shuddered but did not squeal. John cursed himself when he realized he didn't have the bucket positioned properly, and some of the blood spilled onto the planks of the floor.

Once he bled the hog dry, John began making the cuts down the center so that he could strip it of its hide. Though unpracticed, he managed to remove it without too much mess, and from there, he used the knife to saw away the skin from the meat. He acted on instinct rather than experience, and he surprised himself by doing a good job. John imagined the ghost of his grandfather whispering instructions to him, and for all he knew, the old man's spirit inhabited him and worked through him for the duration of the process. This thought gave him pleasure, and in time he began to enjoy himself, even whistling by the time it came time to gut the hog. Only when he had the animal washed down the meat hanging from hooks did he remember to save the heart. He nearly fumbled it, his hands so wet with gore and viscera, so he set it inside the bucket of blood for good safe keeping. Then he returned to the house.

He saw the girl waiting for him outside. He felt a flutter in his chest at the sight of her wearing a t-shirt that belonged to his mother, reaching just far enough to cover her thatch of pubic hair. In his imagination, he saw himself married to her and wondered what she would do if he tried to kiss her.

But she paid him little mind other than to ask, "Where is it?"

He faced the reality that the hunger in her eyes was not for him. He indicated the bucket that swung from his hand, the animal's gore slopping onto the ground. She took it greedily and plunged her hands into it. Out they came with the heart of the beast. He watched as she sat back onto her haunches and bit into it.

John didn't know what he expected. Perhaps he didn't imagine she would cook it, but the sight of her devouring the raw organ left him frozen. When she finished, she smiled at him, her front covered with blood, bits of tissue between her teeth. Surprisingly, his romantic notions did not flee at the sight of her mastication, and part of him still wanted to kiss her.

"You don't have to eat that," he said, doing his upmost to mask his disgust. "Plenty of meat off the carcass."

She paused to wipe her mouth with the back of her arm. Then she used the same blood-smeared arm to point at the bucket. "Take that to the spot where I bled you. Pour it into the earth. I'll bestow more. That'll be my gift."

"What the fuck are you?"

"Just do it and witness for yourself. I'll call forth a flock of chickens. How does that sound?"

He laughed and looked up at the clouds. "Tasty. Why not a cow?"

"You want a whole cow, do you? One you can eat all by yourself?"

John believed he could in fact eat a whole cow by himself. With things becoming scarce, they'd gone so long with so little that he no longer knew what counted as gluttony.

He left her sitting on her haunches, blood-smeared and devouring the remainder of her meal. Once in the pasture, it took him little effort to identify the spot she meant. Tiny flowers sprung up there, and he considered plucking them from the earth and presenting them to her as a gift. Maybe slick his hair back and see if one of his grandfather's button-down shirts fit him. But instead, he followed her instructions, upending the bucket and letting the blood cover the flowers and seep into the ground.

Once he completed the process, he turned to see if he earned the girl's approval. But she no longer sat there.

Instead, he saw the deputy leaning against his vehicle, watching him.

"What you got there, John?" the deputy asked as John returned with the bucket. "That looked like an awful lot of blood."

The bucket's handle felt hot in John's hand. He wondered if he could swing it with enough force to crack the deputy's skull. At least knock him unconscious for a while.

The deputy must have sensed these thoughts because he touched his service pistol as John came closer.

"You housing livestock?" the deputy asked.

John didn't break his stride as he continued to close the distance between them. The deputy walked to the other side of the car, trying to make the move look casual. John continued his march toward the shed.

"If you're harvesting livestock, I need to know," the deputy said.

John stopped and tried to lock eyes with the deputy, but the man's sunglasses made it impossible.

"There a law I'm breaking?" said John.

"It's a local industry. You're stealing from people's livelihoods."

John tried to laugh out loud at this remark, but the sound that existed his throat sounded like a groan—a weak one even to his own ears.

"You ready to return Mr. Randall's property?" asked the deputy as John continued past him toward the shed, no more caution in his voice, apparently certain now that John would not try to bash him in the head.

Only John didn't share the man's confidence. Aware that he shouldn't open the door in the man's presence, he stopped, but he didn't have a chance to answer.

His mother did that for him.

"If Pinky Randall lost something, he can go look for it elsewhere," she said. "Or he can go fuck himself. Tell him I don't much care which."

Turning, the deputy smiled at her. John wondered how many strikes with the metal bucket it would take to see the man's skull. An old commercial jingle ran through his mind.

"You can tell him yourself," the deputy said. "He said no way can you say no to him. He said you don't know the meaning of the word."

"Time to leave, Gerald," said Laura.

John didn't even realize the deputy had a name, and it goaded him to hear his mother use it.

"I almost told Mr. Randall I already knew you couldn't say no, but I thought I ought to keep that as our little secret. A gentleman doesn't talk."

"Go on now," Laura said. "Don't come back."

"Where is that pig I saw earlier? You already slaughter it?" Scanning the area, his eyes fell on the figure who appeared in the doorway to the house—the girl, still wearing a shirt without britches. "Well, hello there. Seems I won't have to send Mr. Randall after all."

He stepped forward, clearly intending to clear a path to the door by pushing Laura aside.

Only he didn't make it far.

John moved faster than the deputy (*Gerald*, he told himself), and with a mighty swing of the bucket, he sent the officer sprawling face first. His victim wore no hat, and from his head erupted a plume of blood. John leaned over and struck him again. In his mind, that old jingle continued to play on repeat. *How many licks does it take...?*

Not two, apparently. John struck a third time.

Though senseless, the law man had not fallen unconscious. He managed to roll over and look at John in mute terror. One of his eyes began filling with blood.

"How many licks does it take?" John said along with the voice in his head, but nothing could drown out his mother, who screamed for him to stop. But he struck again, this time aiming for the deputy's face.

When John lifted the improvised weapon, the deputy's nose appeared comically smaller, reduced to crushed bone and cartilage. Drool flowed from his half-open lips along with tooth fragments. The blood eye came dislodged and lay against his cheek, holding on by a sliver of optic nerve. A horrible gurgling noise arose from the man's throat as he choked on blood and the remains of his teeth.

"Not four licks, that's for sure," John told the voice in his head. "Maybe five?" He may have spoken out loud, but he wasn't sure. For good measure, he brought down the bucket two more times.

Ten

Laura would never unsee her sweet boy obliterating the deputy's face. The vision would haunt her dreams, and during her waking moments, nothing could hold her attention long enough before she squeezed her eyes shut and physically shuddered. Nothing could blot it out, and she could hear that noise he made while inflicting violence. Was he singing? She felt certain she heard him singing as he turned the man's face to pulp. Almost as worse, the sight of her own flesh and blood with that wide-eyed stared, standing over the deputy's immobile form when it finally stopped. She wanted to run away screaming, and it took everything inside her to resist that impulse.

"Give it to me, John," she said afterwards, her voice barely above a whisper. He didn't respond, instead clinging to the bucket as he loomed over the deputy, his breath haggard and heavy.

Only when she gently took the bucket out of John's hand did she realize that the sound of breathing came from the deputy. John barely made a sound, but he released the bucket.

Together, they watched the deputy, her thoughts scrambling over what they ought to do with him, his thoughts indecipherable. Surely, the deputy wouldn't live that much longer, would he? He'd lost both of his eyes, and his nose rammed into his face, Laura didn't know how he could go on breathing. For his sake, she hoped he'd fallen unconscious and could feel nothing, but some part of his brain obviously refused to give up. She noticed that his left hand trembled near his holster, as if he wanted to locate his gun. She considered taking it herself and shooting him.

Before she could act on this impulse, the girl stepped forth from the house.

"Take him into the shed," she said. The command in her voice told Laura that she'd watched the whole thing. "Find a blanket and wrap it around him so he can stay warm."

At first, Laura misunderstood and took her to mean that she intended to nurse the deputy back to health. John obeyed and began dragging the man by his feet. Then the meaning became clear: she wanted to keep the man's circulatory system going for a little while longer. She wanted a warm heart to bite into.

As John completed his task, Laura found herself unable to move. Frozen, she looked at the deputy's car, struggling to come to terms with the fact that they needed to do something about its presence.

She hadn't noticed the flock of hens that gathered in the pasture, their beaks poking at the spot where the pig once rooted. Whatever called forth the swine now called forth the fowl. Laura felt the girl watching her in expectation. For what, she didn't know. Thanks? Praise? Laura could only provide hatred and fear.

"You can keep them for their eggs. Slaughter them now or when they go barren. They'll provide a bounty as long as you keep feeding me," the girl said.

"I ought to kill you." Trembling, Laura could barely form the words.

The girl responded with a chilling smile. She returned to the house as if she owned it. Laura didn't stop her.

Eleven

The girl liked the old woman, her quiet, her warmth. She liked how she could press her body against hers and listen to her heartbeat. She noticed a slight arrhythmia, but she could tell the woman possessed an otherwise strong heart. It responded to her presence by growing more rapid, as if it wanted to leap out of the woman's chest and into her mouth.

"You smell so good," she whispered, curling herself into a fetal position alongside her.

She wondered what this woman would say if the stroke had not robbed her of speech. The blood coursing through her body would have to communicate for her, the veins and arteries swelling and stretching with the rise of blood pressure. Another stroke would finish her for good, so she stroked the woman's chest and cooed for her to breathe more evenly.

She'd taken the form of an elderly woman many times before, crow-faced and wrinkled, offering spells in exchange for gifts. On this land once lived a people who trusted her, saw her age not as infirmity, but as a sign of great wisdom. They knew how to honor her, and their sacrifices came to her willingly, bestowed with ornamental jewelry, and she would sometimes huddle with these sacrifices inside huts made from wood and stone, much like she now did on this bed made for dying, while outside the others danced and celebrated the coming harvest. She experienced true happiness those days, now like now, when the greed of men led to such unflattering treatment.

How long had she been held prisoner? Enough time for her to grow weak with hunger, but now she felt her strength returning. In no time, the mother and her son would let go of their misgivings about her, and they would come to appreciate the bountiful blessings she could provide. No doubt they would enjoy the hens as well as the swine, and she would provide more. Corn once grew on this land, rows and rows of it, and the people ate it and sang songs to her. She answered by providing abundance. In lakes and rivers, now dried up and vanished, she summoned fish to leap into their boats, and everyone was happy.

She thought of the man's heart and how good it would taste. She would reward this offering with a cow. Perhaps two. Later, she would teach them the songs once sung in her glory, though she herself struggled to remember them clearly. Maybe they could invent their own. It didn't matter. Just as long as they provided her with offerings.

Her thoughts wandered as she used a fingernail to trace the circle she created earlier on the old woman's sternum. She would never allow anyone to misuse her or her gifts again. She was meant to feel the sun's rays or stand in fields of dirt as rain fell and soaked the earth. She liked to feel the stirring of growth beneath her feet.

She must have pressed too deeply into the groove of the old woman's flesh, for a trickle of blood appeared. "I'm sorry," she said to the woman who trembled wordlessly against her. She licked her finger clean, then used her tongue on the space between the woman's withered breasts. With the coppery scent came another memory: seeing the younger version of Laura brought into her dungeon by her jailer. She supposed he never intended to feed her, for that moment marked the beginning of her starvation. Instead, he wanted to show her the power he held over her, making her observe the spectacle from the shadows. Indeed, she watched with curiosity as Laura fought and struggled against her assailant. At the time, he still fed her on occasion, and she listened to the beating of their hearts in anticipation of a feast. But she noticed something else too, not quite an additional heartbeat, not yet at least. More like the echo of one from some future place. She realized then that something already grew in that womb her jailer sought to violate, something small, newly formed and barely stirring. Already inclined to reject this meal if he offered it to her, she quietly rejoiced when the girl successfully fought him, kicking him in his naked groin and causing him to curl into a moaning ball of pain. As she watched the girl escape with her dress torn, her face bruised and bleeding, she wondered if she already knew what she carried in her womb.

"Did you know?" She whispered the question to the stricken woman whose bed she now shared. The body next to her shuddered in reply.

She obviously did know, and the girl pondered what a terrible thing that was. An awful secret. She could practically read this elderly mind and see for herself those late nights spent alone in that recliner. Father and daughter. Under this very roof.

Like her, Laura must have felt like a prisoner. Such unexpected ways their destinies intertwined.

The girl broke more skin, this time deliberately, and more blood appeared. She did so without apology.

After this humiliation, her jailer stopped bringing her offerings. In response, the land went into decline. With magical glyphs he learned from his father (who learned them from his own), he kept her bound in that place, until she assumed he'd forgotten all about her. There, she grew hungry and became nostalgic for the songs once sung in her honor.

"I wish you could sing to me," she whispered to the woman, whose heat kept her warm. Again, she heard the heart flutter and felt the body tremble. "Maybe," she said, an idea coming to her, "you can pay your tribute in other ways."

Twelve

The deputy somehow went on breathing, just refusing to die. At one point, Laura prepared a bowl full of broth and brought it to him in the shed, where he lay in the corner underneath a blanket, just as the strange girl instructed. Laura wanted to call for help, but she knew what they would do to John, so she just prayed for the deputy to finally die. Instead, he stubbornly clung to life.

Laura couldn't see how. She tried to feed him the broth with a spoon, but the effort only resulted in a mess. He hardly had a functioning mouth anymore, not after what happened to his jaw under the blows of the bucket.

After nearly giving up, Laura thought she could hear words come out of his mouth. It unnerved her to do so, but she moved her ear closer to where his tongue dangled.

Not talking, she realized. Humming. He was trying to sing.

Laura tried to guess the tune, but she couldn't place it. If she could recognize it, then maybe she could sing it back to him and provide some modicum of comfort. She hoped he made these sounds in a state of unconsciousness, if not sleep, then some approximation of it. How much function remained in his brain, she couldn't guess, but she hoped that the world to him now amounted to a pleasant low-fi dream. Maybe one in which he replayed a song once sung to him by his mother. She tried to match the tune by humming. She never could sing. Whenever she tried to sing to John, he would just cry and cry, so she stopped altogether. Now she tried to sing the deputy (*Gerald,* she reminded herself) into the next world.

Moments later, the girl appeared in the entryway, followed by John. John's hand once more gripped that notorious bucket. Without saying anything to her, he stepped into the shed and began using the bucket to collect the eggs from the chickens now roosting there.

"You can go on," said the girl. She meant the singing. Laura stopped when the others appeared. "Or I can teach you a different song." The girl looked at John, who blushed and went about collecting the eggs, pretending not to hear. "I can teach you both."

"If we sing," Laura said, "will you go away?"

The deputy's distorted song became a gurgle. Once more, Laura shuddered to imagine how much awareness of his surroundings he maintained.

"It's time to get the knife," the girl said to John.

Carefully, so as not to break the eggs, John set the bucket on the floor planks. Laura could sense him hesitating, his eyes daring back and forth between her and the girl.

"Leave it be, John," Laura said. She felt no more aversion to touching the deputy. She pulled him close, keeping his head cradled on her lap. "Nobody's harming this man any further."

John appeared undecided, but his eyes roamed the shed. Roosting on a pile of straw, the hens clucked softly, like a Greek chorus watching events unfold.

"I don't see it," he said.

With those words, Laura's hopes that her son felt some moral ambivalence began to fade.

She was glad she'd hidden the knife.

The girl studied her face in a knowing way. "Don't you like what I've given you? Meat. Fresh eggs."

"You didn't give us these things." Spittle flew from Laura's mouth as she spoke. "You're an abomination. I don't know what you are. Why don't you just leave?"

"You give me what I want," the girl said, "and I'll bestow other gifts. A cow. Would you like that?"

Ignoring them, John lumbered about the shed. He upended a tub of old rags, then a crate filled with ancient paint containers. Biting her lip, Laura watched him. The girl studied her expression. Then as if reading Laura's thoughts, she pointed to a corner. "Under there," she said.

Laura could feel the heat emanating from the deputy's forehead. He began to sing again, and the girl swayed to the melody. John went to the corner and lifted an old gas can. "Found it," he said, lifting the knife from its hiding place.

Crying, Laura tried to ward John away by waving her hand. He paused in his approach, as if waiting for her to say something. When no words materialized, he said, "A cow, Mama. She's going to bring us a *cow*."

Then he straddled the deputy's prone body, and as Laura held the dying man's head, he began cutting out his heart.

Thirteen

The promise of a cow came fulfilled.

The girl ate the deputy's heart in front of them without shame or embarrassment, and afterwards, she instructed them to bury the rest of the body in the pasture, specifying the spot where the other blood fell. John worked by himself into the evening digging the hole, and after filling the earth atop the deputy, he ate a robust meal and eventually fell into a deep sleep.

Before alighting to bed, he told his mother goodnight and professed his love for her, but she said nothing back to him. She seemed disinclined to talk to him anymore, a turn of events he could not have foreseen, especially considering how she'd made him her confidante throughout his life. Even before he could form complete sentences, she would tell him about the misfortunes that befell them, all thanks to that confounded Pinky Randall.

For that reason, he didn't know what to think when he caught his mother singing to that fuckwit deputy (*Gerald*—how he hated that name). The sight of her doing that made him feel like an intruder, and before falling asleep, he tried to recall even one instance where she'd sung to him. Considering he remembered every conversation between them, he doubted she'd ever had done anything like that for him. If he couldn't remember it, it didn't happen. Maybe he didn't possess the highest IQ in the world, but he possessed an unparalleled memory, not counting occasions like leaving behind a tire iron after an act of arson.

These troubling thoughts managed to leave his sleep undisturbed. That night, he dreamed vividly. Some strange shit, too, mostly about the girl. He'd seen her undressed, and he didn't dare touch her, but not so in dreams. There, in the pasture, they laid with one another in his dream, her on top, her pelvis grinding into his. At some point in the dream, he became distracted by a circle of onlookers, men and women with strange clothes and features, all of them singing in a language he couldn't understand. The girl paid them no mind, and after a moment, neither did he. But before they could complete their carnal act, his body began to decay. Soon, he couldn't move, and he relied on her to maintain the rhythm of their coitus. Eventually, his flesh rotted away completely, and only his bones remained. The girl continued to grind until even the bones became dust that dispersed in the wind.

He awoke feeling as if he had not slept at all. Even more hungry than restless, he heard his stomach growl, so he scrambled himself three eggs and he fried bacon. He couldn't think of another time in his life when he could afford himself such a luxury. Hoping the aroma of cooking would attract his mother, he scrambled another egg after wolfing down his first breakfast. When she didn't appear, he ate it himself as he stood near the window. There, he gazed toward the pasture, where he saw it, just like she promised.

A cow.

He smiled and took his time eating, confident he could approach the animal on his own time without fear of scaring it off, just like the others. He washed his plate, scrubbing it completely clean before going off to find a coil of rope. Maybe they would have fresh milk soon. He couldn't see how his mother could go on mourning the deputy when such luxuries waited for them on the horizon.

Surprisingly, the cow did resist him, tossing its neck and running before he could get close enough. His hands fumbled with the rope, too, and despite such a grand beginning to a beautiful morning, he became frustrated. He swore at the cow, as if unkind words would make it stand still.

"Ain't much of a cowboy, I see."

John twisted around at the sound of the voice. He found himself staring at Pinky Randall standing within a few feet of him.

He'd seen Pinky Randall plenty of times, but always at a distance, never this close. Nor had Pinky Randall ever acknowledged his existence before. Seeing him now, so close, caused John to stop his struggles with the cow. Dumbfounded, he stared at his father, who wanted nothing to do with him, and he found himself cataloguing the flaws and imperfections in the man's appearance: the balding head badly disguised with a comb-over, the full belly hanging over the belt loops of his jeans. Such flaws made John realize that despite his justifiable hatred of this man, he had elevated him to a god-like status in his imagination. It took all his inner strength not to kneel in supplication. Something brown marred the side of Pinky Randall's nose, some kind of mole, perhaps even cancerous. How could a man with such grotesque features accrue so much wealth and power? Of course, John knew Pinky inherited everything that belonged to him, and he felt renewed resentment over how those things would never get passed down to him. His lawful birthright. He stood there, hating and worshipping Pinky Randall all at the same time, as if the deity of an unjust existence had just come down from the heavens and stood before him. It dawned on him for the first time that his mother had not only taught him to hate Pinky Randall, but also fear him at the same time.

"Judging by the look of things around here," said Pinky Randall, "I need look no further for what has been taken from me."

The girl, thought John, *he knows she's here.* But he reached deep down into his hatred and drew forth defiance. "I ain't got nothing that belongs to you. I wouldn't *want* what you've got."

Pinky laughed, as if he'd just heard a good one.

"I'm just a businessman who's trying to protect his property. I take it you've got a mind for business, too?"

Wary of trap, John didn't answer.

Pinky sniffed, his eyes scanning the area. "I was going to ask what happened to Deputy Purvis. Judging by the presence of livestock, I don't expect him to be clocking in and reporting for work any time soon."

"No one's seen him," John said. "Couldn't say when or if he'll show up anywhere. If he doesn't, maybe we can get a proper sheriff in this town."

Pinky erupted with laughter. "Boy, you've got a mouth on you. Do you even know who I am?"

John nodded, feeling again that sense of standing in the presence of a deity and hating himself for it. He wondered if the laughter might wake up the rest of the house.

"The people here don't need a sheriff. They have me. I am the law. And that means I can overlook Deputy Purvis' mysterious disappearance." He winked at John's feet and the freshly dug earth of the grave beneath them. "And you're going to need a lot more to keep this up. Once you start, she wants more and more and more. Pretty soon, it gets tiring."

No longer harassed by John, the cow stood still, grazing upon a clump of weeds. Pinky walked toward it, and John noted that the animal didn't run this time, remaining in place and even allowing Pinky to pet it behind its ears. The cow's udders hung heavy and full between its legs, and it seemed to listen as Pinky whispered something to it. Then Pinky removed something from the belt around his waist, something which the overhanging flesh hid from view.

"I could teach you to cowboy," Pinky said. "But as a businessman yourself, I'm sure you understand how rivalry works."

John now saw what he held. A pistol, its barrel pressed to the animal's head. John cried out, and Pinky wavered, turning the pistol in John's direction as if anticipating violence. Instead, he smiled. "Why, hello Laura."

John's mother marched toward them, her mouth stretched as if in preparation of a terrible scream. Her steps slowed when she saw the gun, but her approach continued.

"It's been a long time," said Pinky.

"You need to leave now," she said.

Pinky looked at John. "Which one of you hid Deputy Purvis' vehicle?"

John spoke softly, the words nearly caught in his throat. "She did."

Pinky returned his attention to Laura, who now stood next to John. "Well, that was a piss-poor job. Not far from here, hidden behind a few trees. Did you *want* your son to get caught, Laura?"

John turned to her, curious to hear the answer. He wondered

if he did the wise thing in letting her take care of the car while he disposed of the remains.

"He's *your* son," Laura said, evidently not inclined to answer the real question. John wondered: *did* she want him to get caught and perhaps wind up on Death Row?

Another bellowing round of laughter from Pinky, this time with more contempt. "I don't think so," he said once he could get enough air. To John, he added, "You haven't swallowed that load of horse shit, have you?"

"I don't know," said John. He found himself withering under Pinky's gaze, and he believed him. "No. I don't believe it."

"John," said Laura.

John waited for more, but she had nothing to add.

"Alright, then," Pinky said. "Listen, cowboy, you keep salt inside that house?"

John thought about it. Then he nodded.

"A lot of it?"

John shook his head.

"Well, we're going to need a lot of it, because you're going to salt this earth. All of it. And I'm going to come back and make sure you did it." He lifted the pistol, and for a moment, John thought he planned on shooting his mother. He tried to position himself to shield her, but it turned out that Pinky had other ideas.

With methodical precision, he placed the barrel between the cow's eyes and shot it dead.

They all watched it shudder once before its legs folded, causing it to fall to the earth.

"You'll want to bury that first," Pinky said, still gripping the pistol.

John watched as heat rose like steam from the expiring animal.

The shot still ringing in his ears, he finally dropped to his knees, but he did so in order to press his head against its hide, hoping to conceal his tears. He also wanted to listen for signs of life within the cow, wondering if he could use his cutting skills to rescue a calf in its womb before it died, too.

But he heard nothing. Instead he felt Pinky's hand on his back. "There, there," Pinky Randall said. "Stand up like a man. Not just for your mother, but for your grandmother, too. I see the gunshot has roused her from the house."

Confused, John looked up and saw his grandmother approaching them.

Laura saw, too. Her mouth hung open in a struggle to put disbelief into words. The woman had shown no signs of recovery and had not walked in years, but she appeared strong in her bearing, her face no longer showing the effects of the stroke that debilitated her.

"Gracey, it has been a long time," Pinky Randall said. "I've not seen you since Ralph's funeral. I heard that you weren't well, so it's a pleasure to see you looking so spry."

He let his arms hang at his side, as if he anticipated a hug from the woman who did answer or break her stride. Instead, Gracey walked past him and knelt next to John. She placed her hand on the cow and looked at John.

"There will be another one. You watch and see," she said, her voice barely worn around the edges, not at all like that of a woman unused to speaking.

John studied her face through the tears that marred his vision. He struggled to remember how she looked and sounded before the stroke. Not like the woman he saw now. He could recall that much. Her eyes looked big and dark, unmarred by cataracts or any other sign of age.

"Gracey," said Pinky Randall, "there's evidently some controversy regarding the paternity of this young man. Perhaps you can put the boy's mind to rest. Am I his father?"

Still regarding John, his grandmother said, "No."

"There you have it," said Pinky. "Laura, even your own mother says you're a liar."

"Goddamn you," said Laura, quietly at first, as if speaking to herself, but then she repeated the words loud enough for all the heavens to hear. That seemed to open the floodgates of repressed rage, and with each word she spoke to her mother, her voice rose in volume, eventually growing as loud as thunder. "You let it happen. You knew it was happening. *You just did nothing.*"

The final sound that escaped her throat came out as a sob, and John thought she'd exhausted her rage. But then Laura fell upon the old woman, biting, tearing, clawing. His grandmother did not fight back, either from surprise or because she'd resolved to let her own daughter tear her apart. Someone laughed, probably Pinky Randall, though John couldn't swear that the laughter didn't come from himself. His own actions seemed to occur without his volition.

Like grabbing the gun from Pinky. Or maybe Pinky handed it to him. He couldn't remember. He could hardly recall firing it three times.

The first shot hit his mother in the back. She turned, looking at him with an expression of surprise and betrayal. Or maybe she didn't recognize him. Whatever the case, John barely recognized himself anymore. He liked to think that his finger just slipped the second time, when the bullet hit her shoulder. She held up her good arm, like she intended to reach out to him. She took one step in his direction, but the third shot ripped through her skull, and she dropped like a sack of potatoes.

"I would bury her over here, too," said Pinky Randall, "and I highly recommend you do it *before* you salt the earth."

The vision of his mother went blurry, and only after a moment did John realize that was because he was crying. He felt Pinky Randall take the pistol from his hand, and he offered no resistance.

Once more, Pinky patted him on the shoulder, but it brought no consolation. "I do want what belongs to me. I expect she's in the house."

John and his grandmother followed Pinky toward the entrance. As they passed the shed and heard the sound of the chickens, Pinky instructed him that they would all have to be destroyed, too, along with any eggs they left behind. The man walked ahead of them without fear, arms swinging in confidence that John either would not or could not inflict any harm upon him. Eventually, they came to the grandmother's room, and if Pinky demonstrated no surprise at what they found, other than to say, "Well, I'll be."

The girl's body appeared mummified, its brown flesh brittle and flaking. It huddled there in the middle of the bed, legs pulled up in a fetal position, one thumb in its mouth as if it tried to suckle before it died. From all appearances, that death occurred a millennia ago. John babbled something, as if someone compelled him to explain the impossible. Pinky told him to shut up. John's grandmother stood behind them both, observing.

"Well, good riddance," Pinky said. "This goes in the hole, too. Show me where you keep the salt. You're going to need a lot of it."

Fourteen

As it happened, John did not own enough salt to get the job done, so Pinky explained that he would return later with what they needed. "You killed the only man I trusted," Pinky said, "so you're going to have to do all this work by yourself. I'll expect you not to tax your grandmother by making her assist you in any way. The good woman has been through enough in her lifetime."

Pinky paused, observing the effect of this speech on John's grandmother. If he expected praise or thanks or an offer of iced tea, he received none of these things. If, like John, he noticed something strange about her eyes, he gave no indication of that either. The two of them watched mutely as Pinky pulled his bulk into his pink convertible. Before driving away, Pinky pointed his finger at John. "I want that hole completed before I get back later. Everything done the way I told you. You hear me?"

John didn't answer. He just stared at this man he once thought of as his distant father.

Still, Pinky nodded as if John said something that met his approval. "You do a good job, and I'll give you a job. There's an opening, I hear. Maybe you'll make deputy eventually." And then he roared away in a cloud of dust.

John spent the rest of the morning digging. Not surprisingly, he struggled over how to move the cadaver of the cow. Eventually, he got the idea of using the rope to tie it to the bumper of the car and using that to move it, but he only succeeded in pulling off the bumper. Exhausted and barren of ideas, he sat on the ground next to his mother's corpse and once more began to cry. After some time of that, he looked up to discover his grandmother watching.

"I expect that you'll be asking for her heart," John said.

His grandmother smiled. "No. She's been through too much. She gets to keep her heart."

John nodded and wiped away his tears. He wanted to take it back, take everything back. Later, when he finished his task, he would take his grandmother to the site of Ralph Teecar's burial site, and he would smash that lying grave marker in front of her. He would reduce it to rubble. He might even piss on the grave. He would tell her all the facts about his existence that he'd put together in just that little while, but he suspected she already somehow knew.

Giving up on the cow for the time being, he went inside the house and carried the mummified corpse of the girl outside. Bits of her came apart during the process, and it took him more time than he expected to make sure he got everything. He carried the body to the hole, cradled like a baby. Behind him, his grandmother followed, carrying a foot that fell off some distance back. Delicately, so as not to disturb any more of her remains, he lifted the body into the hole. Then he did the same to his mother, positioning the bodies so that they lay side by side. Afterwards, he looked down upon his work, wondering if he ought to say something.

Standing next to him, his grandmother spoke instead.

"I am hungry, though," she said. "Starving, in fact."

He nodded. He knew what she liked to eat. He marked the hour and calculated how long it might take for Pinky Randall to return with his supplies. He thought of how he bled the hog suspended by his ankles, and he thought of how the same process should work just fine again. One last slaughter, he thought.

Then his grandmother said, "I'll bestow plenty more gifts after that."

Okay, he decided, maybe not the very last.

About the Author

Douglas Ford's short fiction has appeared in a variety of anthologies, magazines, and podcasts, as well as two collections, *Ape in the Ring and Other Tales of the Macabre and Uncanny* and *The Infection Party and Other Stories of Dis-Ease.* His longer works include *The Beasts of Vissaria County* and *The Trick.* His novella, *Little Lugosi (A Love Story)* won the Literary Nastie award for best long fiction in 2022. He lives on the west coast of Florida.

You can connect with me on:

 https://douglasfordwrites.com
 https://www.facebook.com/profile.php?id=100064149938106